EDWARD'S EXPLOIT
and Other Thomas the Tank Engine Stories

Based on *The Railway Series* by t̶ ̶

Photographs by David Mitton and Terry Permane
for Britt Allcroft's production of *Thomas the Tank Engine and Friends*

A Random House PICTUREBACK®

Library of Congress Cataloging-in-Publication Data
Edward's exploit and other Thomas the tank engine stories / photographs by David Mitton and Terry Permane for Britt Allcroft's production of Thomas the tank engine and friends. p. cm. — (A Random House pictureback) "Based on The Railway series by the Rev. W. Awdry." Summary: Sir Topham Hatt's engines learn that they get the most accomplished when they work together. ISBN 0-679-83896-1 (trade pbk.) [1. Railroads—Trains—Fiction. 2. Behavior—Fiction.] I. Mitton, David, ill. II. Permane, Terry, ill. III. Awdry, W. Railway series. IV. Thomas the tank engine and friends.
PZ7.E2655 1993 [E]—dc20 92-23189
Manufactured in the United States of America 10 9 8 7 6 5

RANDOM HOUSE 🏠 NEW YORK

Donald and Douglas

Donald and Douglas are twins and had arrived from Scotland to help Sir Topham Hatt—but only one engine had been expected.

The twins meant well, but did cause confusion. Sir Topham Hatt had given them numbers—Donald 9 and Douglas 10—but he was still planning to send one engine home.

There was a brake-van in the yard that had taken a dislike to Douglas. Things always went wrong when he had to take it out. His trains were late, and he was blamed. Douglas began to worry.

Donald, his twin, was angry. "You're a muckle nuisance," said Donald. "It's to leave ye behind I'd be wanting."

"You can't," said the brake-van. "I'm essential."

"Och, are you?" Donald burst out. "You're nothing but a screechin' and a noise when all is said and done. Spite Dougie, would you? Take that."

"Oh! Ooh!" cried the van.

"There's more coming should you misbehave."

The van behaved better after that.

Until one day Donald had an accident. The rails were slippery. He couldn't stop in time.

Donald wasn't hurt, but Sir Topham Hatt was most annoyed. "I am disappointed, Donald. I didn't expect such—um—clumsiness from you. I had decided to send Douglas back and keep you."

"I'm sorry, sir," said Donald.

"I should think so too. You have upset my arrangements. Now James will have to help with the goods work while you have your tender mended. James won't like that."

Sir Topham Hatt was right. James grumbled dreadfully about his extra work.

"Anyone would think," said Douglas, "that Donald had had his accident on purpose. I heard tell about an engine and some tar wagons."

"Shut up!" said James. "It's not funny." He didn't like to be reminded of his own accident.

"Well, well, well. Surely, James, it wasn't you?—You didn't say!"

James didn't say. He slouched sulkily away.

"James is cross," snickered the spiteful brake-van. "We'll try to make him crosser still!"

"Hold back!" giggled the freight cars to each other.

James did his best, but he was exhausted when they reached Edward's station. Luckily Douglas was there.

"Help me up the hill, please," panted James. "These freight cars are playing tricks."

"We'll show them," said Douglas.

Slowly but surely, the snorting engines forced the freight cars up the hill.

But James was losing steam. "I can't do it. I can't do it!"

"Leave it to me!" shouted Douglas.

The conductor was anxious. "Go steady! The van's breaking."

The van was in pieces.

No one had been hurt, and soon Edward came to clear the mess. Sir Topham Hatt was on board. "I might have known it would be Douglas!" he said.

"Douglas was grand, sir," said Edward. "James had no steam left, but Douglas worked hard enough for three. I heard him from my yard."

"Two would have been enough," said Sir Topham Hatt. "I want to be fair, Douglas, but I don't know. I really don't know."

Sir Topham Hatt was making up his mind about which engine to send away—but that's another story. ◉

The Deputation

Snow came early to the Island of Sodor. It was heavier than usual. Most engines hate snow. Donald and Douglas were used to it. Coupled back to back with a van between their tenders and a snowplow on their fronts, they set to work.

They puffed backwards and forwards patrolling the line. Generally, the snow slipped away easily, but sometimes they found deeper drifts.

Presently, they came to a drift which was larger than most. They charged it, and were just backing for another try, when...

"Help! Help!"

"Losh sakes, Donald, it's Henry! Don't worry yourself, Henry. Wait a while. We'll have you out!"

Henry was very grateful. He saw all was not well.

The twins were looking glum. They told him Sir Topham Hatt was making a decision. "He'll send us away for sure."

"It's a shame!" said Percy.

"A lot of nonsense about a broken signalbox," grumbled Gordon.

"That spiteful brake-van too," put in James. "Good riddance. That's what I say."

"The twins were splendid in the snow," added Henry. "It isn't fair." They all agreed that Something Must Be Done, but none knew what.

Percy decided to talk to Edward about it. "What you need," said Edward, "is a deputation." He explained what that was.

Percy ran back quickly. "Edward says we need a depot-station."

"Of course," said Gordon, "the question is..."

"...what is a desperation?" asked Henry.

"It's when engines tell Sir Topham Hatt something's wrong," said Percy.

"Did you say 'tell Sir Topham Hatt'?" asked Duck thoughtfully. There was a long silence.

"I propose," said Gordon, "that Percy be our—er—hum—disputation."

"Me?" squeaked Percy. "I can't."

"Rubbish, Percy," said Henry. "It's easy."

"That's settled then," said Gordon.

Poor Percy wished it wasn't.

"Hello, Percy! It's nice to be back."

Percy jumped. "Er, y-y-yes, sir, please, sir."

"You look nervous, Percy. What's the matter?"

"Please, sir, they've made me a desperation, sir. To speak to you, sir. I don't like it, sir."

Sir Topham Hatt pondered. "Do you mean a deputation, Percy?"

"Yes, sir, please, sir. It's Donald and Douglas. They say, sir, that if you send them away, sir, well, they'll be turned into scrap, sir. That would be dreadful, sir. Please, sir, don't send them away."

"Thank you, Percy. That will do."

Later, Sir Topham Hatt spoke to the engines. "I had a deputation. I understand your feelings, and I've given a lot of thought to the matter."

He paused impressively. "Donald and Douglas, I hear that your work in the snow was good. You shall have a new coat of paint."

The twins were surprised. "Thank ye, sir."

"But your names will be painted on you. We'll have no more 'mistakes.'"

"Thank ye, sir. Does this mean that the both of us…?"

Sir Topham Hatt smiled. "It means—"

But the rest of his speech was drowned in a delighted chorus of cheers and whistles. The twins were here to stay. ◉

The Diseasel

Bill and Ben are tank engine twins. Each has four wheels, a tiny chimney and dome, and a small, squat cab. Their freight cars are filled with china clay. It is needed for pottery, paper, paint, and many other things.

The twins are now kept busy pulling the cars for engines on the main line—and for ships in the harbor.

One morning, they arranged some cars and went away for more.

They returned to find them all gone. The twins were most surprised.

Their drivers examined a patch of oil. "That's diesel," they said.

"It's a what'll?" asked Bill.

"A diseasel, I think," replied Ben. "There's a notice about them in our shed."

"'Coughs and sneezles spread diseasels.' You had a cough in your smoke box yesterday. It's your fault the diseasel came."

"It isn't."

"It is."

"Stop arguing, you two," laughed their drivers. "Let's go and rescue our freight cars."

Bill and Ben were horrified. "But the diseasel will magic us away, like the freight cars."

"He won't magic us," replied their drivers. "We'll more likely magic him. Listen—he doesn't know you're twins. So we'll take away your names and numbers, and then this is what we'll do…"

Puffing hard, the twins set off on their journey to find the diesel. They were looking forward to playing tricks on him.

Creeping into the yard, they found the diesel on a siding with the missing cars. Ben hid behind, but Bill went boldly alongside.

The diesel looked up. "Do you mind?"

"Yes," said Bill. "I do. I want my cars back."

"These are mine," said the diesel. "Go away."

Bill pretended to be frightened. "You're a big bully," he whimpered. "You'll be sorry." He ran back and hid behind the cars on the other side.

Ben now came forward.

"Car stealer!" hissed Ben.

He ran away too.

Bill took his place.

This went on and on till the diesel's eyes nearly popped out.

"Stop! You're making me giddy."

The two engines gazed at him.

"Are there two of you?"

"Yes, we're twins."

"I might have known it."

Just then Edward bustled up. "Bill and Ben, why are you playing here?"

"We're not playing," protested Bill.

"We're rescuing our cars," squeaked Ben. "Even you don't take our cars without asking, but this diseasel did."

"There's no cause to be rude," said Edward severely. "This engine is a Metropolitan Vickers Diesel-Electric, Type 2."

The twins were most impressed. "We're sorry, Mr. —er..."

"Never mind," the diesel smiled. "Call me Boco. I'm sorry I didn't understand about the cars."

"That's all right then," said Edward. "Now off you go, Bill and Ben. Fetch Boco's cars—then you take this lot.

"There's no real harm in them," he said to Boco, "but they're maddening at times."

Boco chuckled. "'Maddening,'" he said, "is the word." **O**

Edward's Exploit

Bertie the Bus was giving some visitors a tour of the Island of Sodor.

It was their last afternoon, and Edward was preparing to take them to meet Bill and Ben.

He found it hard to start the heavy train.

"Did you see him straining?" asked Henry.

"Positively painful," remarked James.

"Just pathetic," grunted Gordon. "He should give up and be preserved before it's too late."

"Shut up!" burst out Duck. "You're all jealous. Edward's better than any of you."

"You're right, Duck," said Boco. "Edward's old, but he'll surprise us all."

"I've done it! We're off! I've done it! We're off!" said Edward as he finally puffed out of the station.

Bill and Ben were delighted to see the visitors. They loved being photographed.

Later they took the party to the China Clay Works in a "brake-van special."

Everyone had a splendid time, and the visitors were most impressed.

Then Edward took the visitors home.

On the way, the weather changed. Wind and rain buffeted Edward. His sanding gear failed, and his fireman rode in front dropping sand on the rails by hand.

Suddenly, Edward's wheels slipped fiercely, and with a shrieking crack, something broke.

The crew inspected the damage. Repairs took some time.

"One of your crankpins broke, Edward," said his driver.

"We've taken your side rods off. Now you're like an old-fashioned engine. Can you get these people home? They must start back tonight."

"I'll try, sir," promised Edward.

Edward puffed and pulled his hardest, but his wheels kept slipping and he could not start the heavy train. The passengers were anxious.

The driver, fireman, and conductor went along the train making adjustments between the coaches.

"We've loosened the couplings, Edward. Now you can pick your coaches up one by one, just as you do with freight cars."

"That'll be much easier," said Edward. "Come...on!" he puffed, and moved cautiously forward. The first coach moving helped to start the second, and the second helped the third.

"I've done it! I've done it!" puffed Edward.

"Steady, boy!" warned his driver. "Well done, boy! You've got them! You've got them!"

And he listened happily to Edward's steady beat as he forged slowly but surely ahead.

At last, battered, weary, but unbeaten, Edward steamed in.

Henry was waiting for the visitors with the Special Train. "Peep! Peep!"

Sir Topham Hatt angrily pointed to the clock, but excited passengers cheered and thanked Edward, his driver, and fireman.

Duck and Boco saw to it that Edward was left in peace. Gordon and James remained respectfully silent. ◉